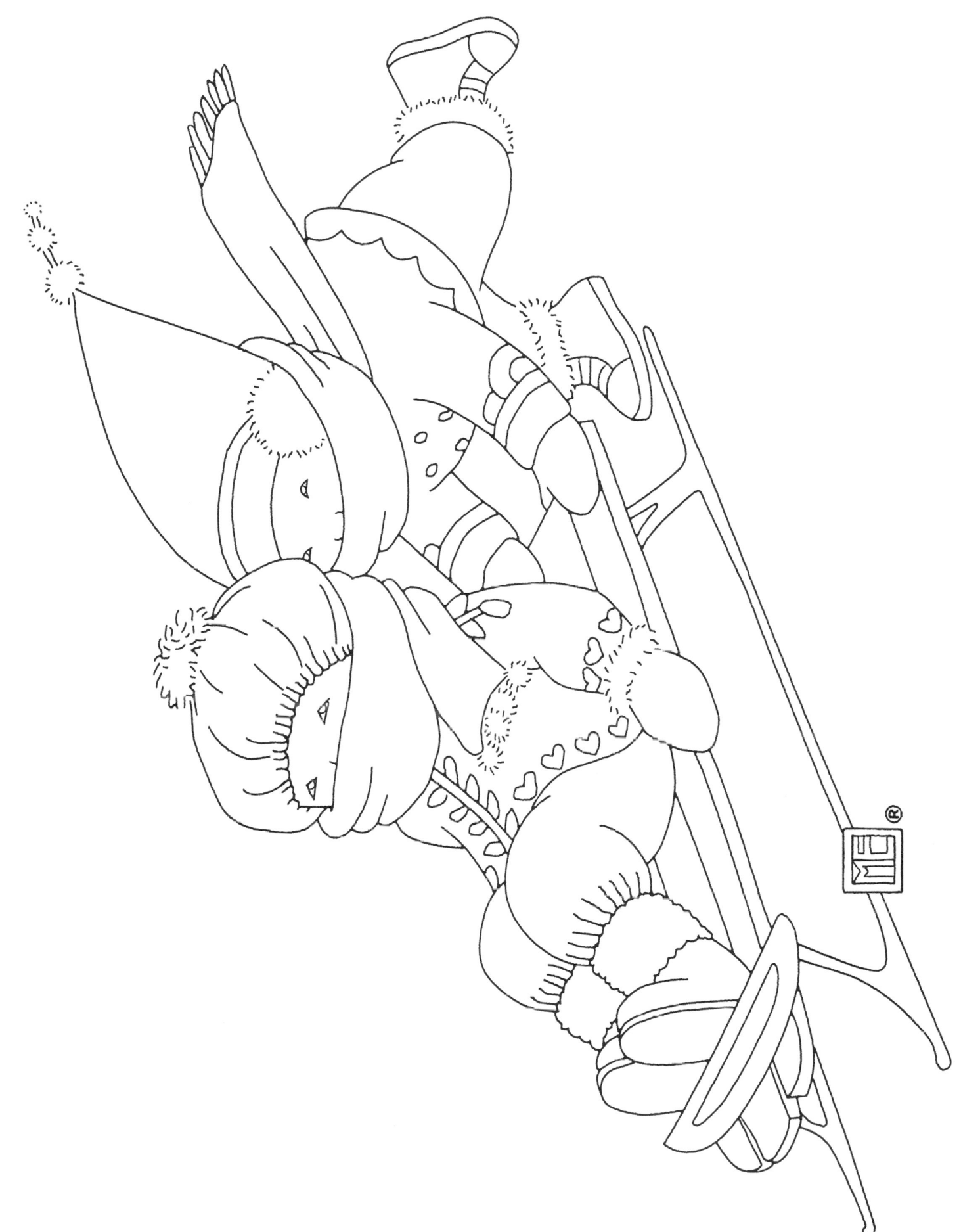

BLESSED IS THE SEASON
WHICH ENGAGES THE WHOLE WORLD
IN A CONSPIRACY OF LOVE

Hamilton Wright Mabie

ALL THE HAPPINESS
YOU CAN HANDLE...

DON'T GET YOUR TINSEL IN A TANGLE!

CHRISTMAS
a time for Sharing

THERE IS SO MUCH GOODNESS IN EACH OF US

THAT IF WE COULD SEE IT GLOW, IT WOULD LIGHT THE WORLD

....SAM FRIEND....

MERRY CHRISTMAS

WAITING FOR THE HOLIDAYS

E IS FOR ELF.

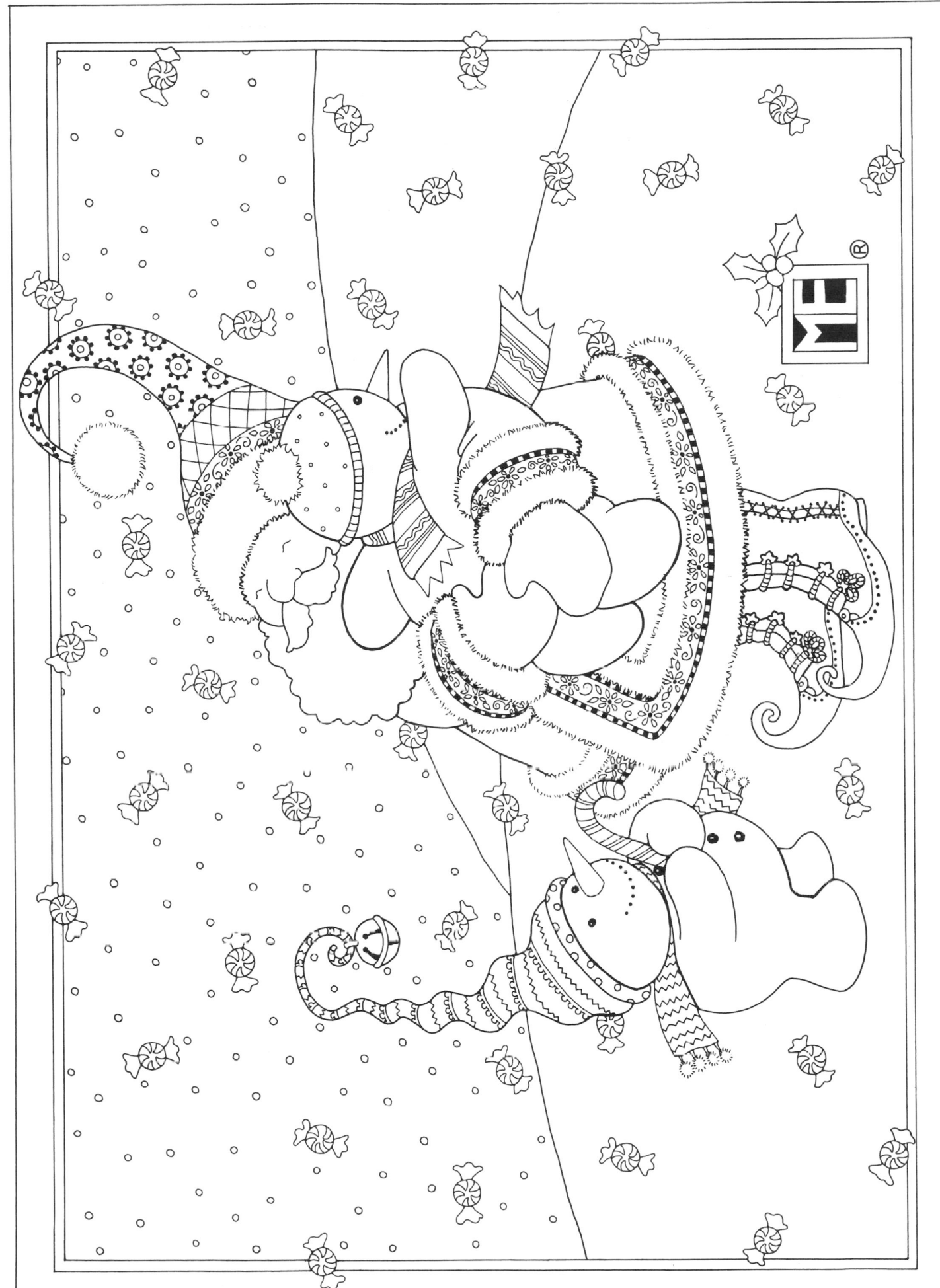

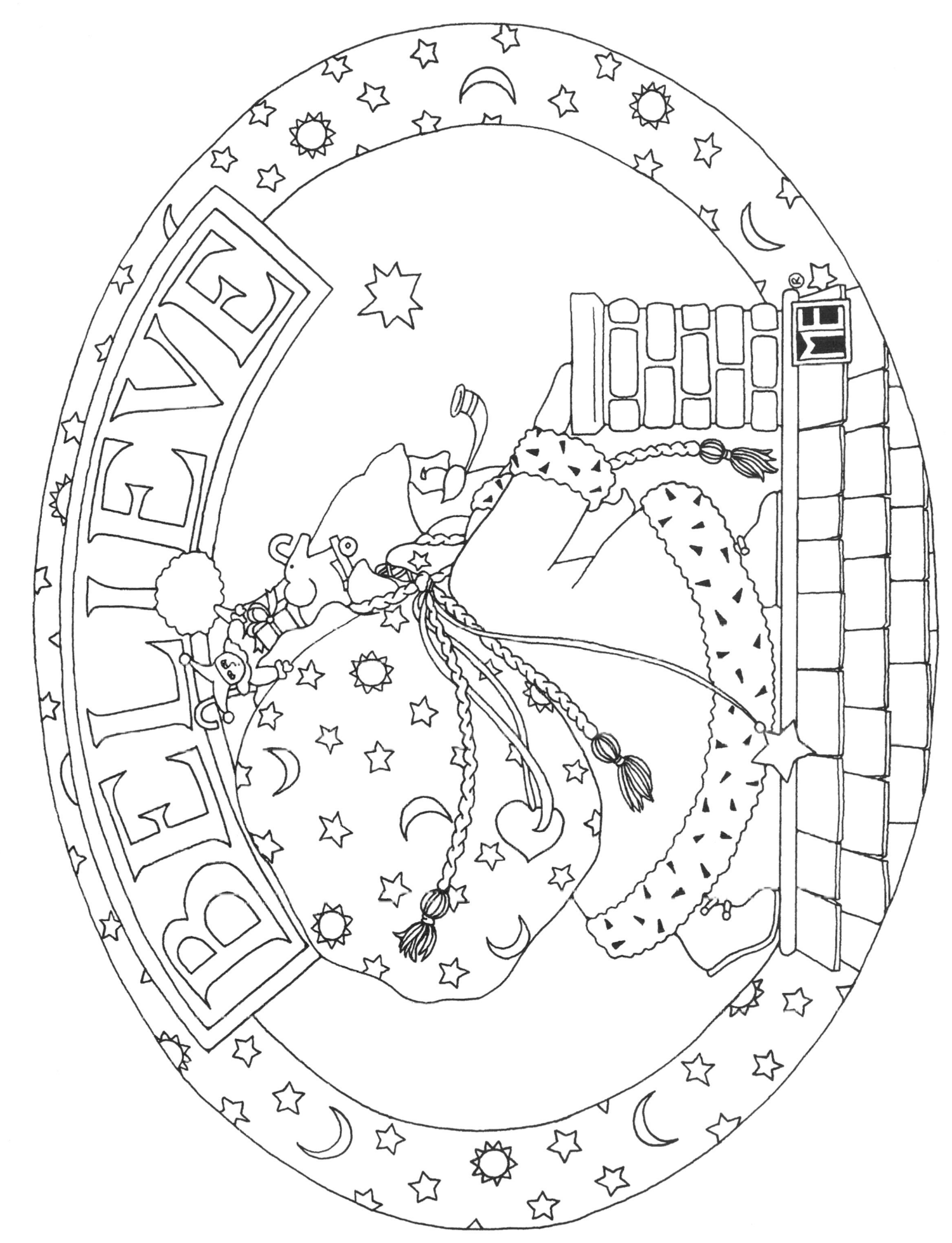